Twentieth Century Fox Home Entertainment
P.O. Box 900
Beverly Hills, CA 90213

Fifth Edition: October 2014

The characters and events portrayed in this book are fictitious.
Although it is based on true events, the narrative is a work of fiction and
further similarities to real persons, living or dead, is coincidental and not
intended by the author.

Elliott, Rand and Marybeth.
Amazing Amy: Tattle Tale / by Rand and Marybeth Elliott, Ph.D;
illustrated by Kirk Van Wormer — 1st ed.
p. cm.
Summary: Amazing Amy embarks on a life lesson teaching it is
better to be true to yourself, doing what you know is right,
than to succumb to peer pressure.
ISBN 584-0-268-252591-2
[1. Morality plays — Fiction. 2. School adventures — Fiction.
3. Pets and children — Fiction] Elliott, Rand and Marybeth

200761509241997

10 9 8 7 6 5 4 3 2 1

NK / CLH

Printed in the United States of America

*To our most darling Amy, light of our lives!
You are the reason, because of your
example, so many children will know
doing what's right can never be wrong!*

How exciting!

Another beautiful day
and who knows what
adventures there might be?

Amy couldn't *wait*
to get to school.

Sorry, Puddles, there
is no time to play.

Amy knew she couldn't
be late for school, she
wanted to win another
'Perfect Attendance' award
for her parents.

She had to hurry.
Amy *never* missed the
school bus.

Oh, no!
Mother's favorite vase!

Oh dear!

Amy knew that it just
wasn't right for Doris,
the housekeeper, to take the
blame for her accident.

But, what would
her parents say?

Amy did not want to
disappoint them.

What a terrible way
to start the day, but the
school bus was waiting...

Amy could not get the image of
her parents scolding Doris
out of her head.

How could she spend the entire
day at school wondering if
she had been wrong?

Today was the day of the big test.
Amy had so much on her mind!

With a deep breath, she knew it
was just one of those days when
she had to try so very hard
to be the *amazing* Amy
she knew she was.

First was the big test.

Amy had practiced all weekend.
Teacher would be so impressed!

Was Danny trying to
copy her paper?

It wasn't fair that Amy had
worked so hard studying
while Danny had
goofed off instead.

He should *not* take credit
for her work.

Thank goodness the
test was over!

It was wrong for Danny to
try to copy her work.

But if she spoke up
and got Danny in trouble,
what would everyone think?

She would not get invited to any
birthday parties!

No one would choose her for their
team in gym class.
Amy was always picked first!

At least she got to see Mr. Turtle
in her next class...

Mr. Turtle was hungry.

It was Brian's day to feed him,
but Amy didn't mind.
Everybody deserved a turn!

Wait! That was *way* too much
food for Mr. Turtle.
Brian should know better.

Amy decided to ask her friend
to stop. Brian seemed upset
by her advice.

She didn't mean to make him
mad, she just wanted to help.

Amy was still thinking about
Doris, Danny, and now Brian,
when her classmate, Joanne,
confronted her in the hall.

Amy did not understand why
Joanne always seemed to dislike
Amy. Amy wanted to be
liked by everyone!

Joanne said to Amy,
*If you tell on Brian, everyone
will know. You're just jealous
because it wasn't your day
to feed Mr. Turtle.*

Why would anyone be mad at her
for telling the truth?

Maybe Amy should ask Suzy
what she thinks she should do…

Suzy was a good friend to Amy,
and always shared her dessert
at lunch, but she seemed afraid
of the other kids!

Suzy looked worried.
She suggested Amy not tell on
Brian because everyone might
call her a *tattletale*.

Amy didn't know what to do!

She thought about what her classmates had said, and how unfair they were being.

She worried Brian would not speak to her. Danny would be mean to her. Joanne would say, *I told you so.* Suzy looked up to Amy. Would she think less?

Amazing Amy realized they *all* seemed to want her to do the wrong thing.

Amy knew right from wrong.
Despite what her deceitful peers
might think, there was only
one thing to do:

She would report to teacher what
Danny, then Brian, had done.
Teacher would be angry when Amy
explained how they had all tried to
bully her into doing the wrong thing.

Then, when she got home,
Amy would tell her parents
the truth about the vase!

Of course, she was making
the right decision.

Even the principal stopped Amy on
her way out the door from school,
to praise her actions.

He told the other kids that they
could *not* ignore her in gym class.
They could *not* exclude her from
their birthday parties.

Not every student would be
brave enough to do as she did;
and they should admire her!

Amy couldn't wait to get home
and tell her parents how
sorry she was. She was ready
to accept responsibility
for breaking the vase.

She would let her parents know that
Amy... *Amazing Amy*...
had the strength and the bravery
to do what her peers could not.
Just like a grown-up!

And look! Even Puddles was happy
to see her. Everything was going
to be just fine.

Better than fine!

With Puddles close at foot,
Amy ran inside.

Without hesitation,
Amy told her parents the truth:

Doris wasn't to blame!
Puddles had broken the
vase that morning while
they had been playing.

Amy understood it was wrong
to let the housekeeper take
the blame, but disappointing her
parents would be just as wrong.

Then she told them all about her
troublesome day at school,
but that by the end, even the
principal had praised her.

Oh, Amy!

Her parents explained
they could never be mad at her
for doing the right thing.

They were so proud Amy
had shown what wonderful
parents she had.

Amy was so brave for facing
down her fears
and taking responsibility!

Just like they had taught her.

She had worried all day
for nothing!

Confronting her fear and telling
the truth had proved what she had
suspected all day...

**When you know what's right
in your heart, listen to your
parents and tell adults the truth,
you can *never* be wrong.**

And that was *AMAZING*...
just like AMY!

Rand and **Marybeth Elliott** are college sweethearts and trained clinical child psychologists. Their immensely successful *Amazing Amy* book series has sold more than a million copies worldwide and received the Pewter Book Prize, the American Society of School Librarians Gold Seal of Approval, and the Parents for Positivity Award. The Elliotts live in New York City where they raise their daughter, Amy, the inspiration for everything they do.

Kirk Van Wormer is an Emmy Award-winning illustrator and storyboard artist. When not working on the adventures of Amazing Amy, he spends his days working from his New York studio, making fish for his two black cats and tending to his overgrown herb garden.

Praise for *Amazing Amy: Tattle Tale*
Pewter Book Prize winner
A top ten children's book pick

"A morality play that will teach future generations of children the difference between 'right' and 'wrong.'"
— PUBLISHERS BI-QUARTERLY

"You can never be wrong, by picking Amazing Amy!*"*
— MADELEINE HOLMS, PARENTS FOR POSITIVITY